ALL IN THE WOODLAND EARLY

ALL IN THE WOODLAND EARLY

An ABC Book

By Jane Yolen   Illustrations by Jane Breskin Zalben

Music and Lyrics by the author

BOYDS MILLS PRESS

*The artist, author, and publishers wish to express their
special thanks to the Children's Librarians of the
Port Washington Public Library for their assistance
with the research for this book.*

Text and music copyright © 1979 by Jane Yolen
Illustrations copyright © 1979 by Jane Breskin Zalben
All rights reserved
Originally published by William Collins Publishers, Inc., and
    Putnam Publishing Group
Boyds Mills Press, Inc.
A Highlights Company
815 Church Street
Honesdale, Pennsylvania 18431
Printed in China

Publisher Cataloging-in-Publication Data
Yolen, Jane
    All in the woodland early: an ABC book/by Jane Yolen; illustrations by Jane Breskin Zalben.
32 p. : col. ill.; cm.
    Includes musical score.
Summary: A woodland hunt reveals animals from A to Z.
Originally published by William Collins, New York.
Hardcover ISBN 1-878093-2   Paperback ISBN 1-56397-645-5
[1. Alphabet. 2. Animals—Fiction.] I. Zalben, Jane Breskin, ill. II. Title.
[E]   1991
LC Card Number 91-70415
First Boyds Mills Press Paperback Edition, 1997

Paperback 10 9 8 7 6 5 4 3 2

To Alexander,
who is learning his ABC's

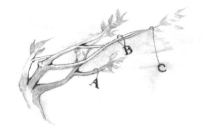

One morning, one morning, one morning in May,
    All in the woodland early,
I saw a young fellow a-making his way
    All in the woodland early.
And where are you going so early today?
"I'm going a-hunting," was all he would say,
    All in the woodland early.

I saw an ANT running,
I saw a black BEAR,
    All in the woodland early;

I saw a small CHIPMUNK,
I saw a brown DEER,
  All in the woodland early.

I saw a swift EAGLE,
A FOX in his lair,
I saw a fine GOOSE,
And I saw a young HARE,
  All in the woodland early.
And where are you going this morning in May?
"We're going a-hunting," was all they would say.

I saw a green INCHWORM
Upon a green tree,
   All in the woodland early;
A JAY on one limb
Started screaming at me,
   All in the woodland early.

I saw a KINGSNAKE
And a LYNX running fast,
A MOUSE and a MINK
Blinked as *they* hurried past,
    All in the woodland early.

And where are you going this morning in May?
"We're going a-hunting," was all they would say.

I saw a shy NEWT;
An OPOSSUM played dead,
All in the woodland early.

A PHEASANT and PARTRIDGE
Flew right past my head,
All in the woodland early.

I heard a loud QUAIL
As he took to his wings,
I saw a young RACCOON
And counted his rings,
    All in the woodland early.

And where are you going this morning in May?
"We're going a-hunting," was all they would say.

I saw a striped SKUNK
And I saw a small SHREW,
    All in the woodland early;
A TURKEY came trotting
Right into my view,
    All in the woodland early.

I saw an URBANUS,

A velvety VOLE,

And a very young WOODCHUCK
Just leaving his hole,
　　All in the woodland early.

And where are you going this morning in May?
"We're going a-hunting," was all they would say.

I saw XYLEBORUS
Upon a tall tree,
  All in the woodland early;

I heard YELLOW JACKET
A-buzzing near me,
  All in the woodland early.

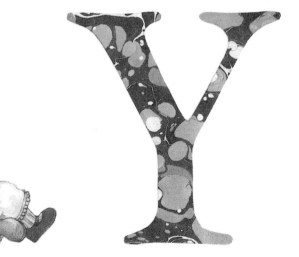

And last of all, ZEMMI,
Who's usually slow,
Ran out and went with them—
But where did they go,
   All in the woodland early?

"Hunting, we're hunting," I heard them all say.
How *can* you go hunting on such a fine day?

"We're hunting for *friends!* Won't you come out and play,
   All in the woodland early?"

All In The Woodland Early

With a bounce

J. Yolen

One morn-ing, one morn-ing, one morn-ing in May,

All in the wood-land ear - ly, I saw a young fel-low a-

mak-ing his way. All in the wood-land ear - ly. And

where are you go-ing so ear-ly to-day? I'm go-ing a-hunt-ing was

all he would say. All in the wood-land ear - ly.

rit.

Music and Lyrics by

Jane Yolen

❧

(To be sung)

One morning, one morning, one morning in May,
All in the woodland early,
I saw a young fellow a-making his way
All in the woodland early.
And where are you going so early today?
"I'm going a-hunting," was all he would say,
All in the woodland early.

(To be sung)
I saw an ANT running,
I saw a black BEAR,
All in the woodland early;
I saw a small CHIPMUNK,
I saw a brown DEER,
All in the woodland early.
I saw a swift EAGLE,
A FOX in his lair,
I saw a fine GOOSE,
And I saw a young HARE,
All in the woodland early.

(To be spoken, rhythmically)
And where are you going this morning in May?
"We're going a-hunting," was all they would say.

(To be sung)
I saw a green INCHWORM
Upon a green tree,
All in the woodland early;
A JAY on one limb
Started screaming at me,
All in the woodland early.
I saw a KINGSNAKE
And a LYNX running fast,
A MOUSE and a MINK
Blinked as *they* hurried past,
All in the woodland early.

(To be spoken)
And where are you going this morning in May?
"We're going a-hunting," was all they would say.

(To be sung)
I saw a shy NEWT,
An OPOSSUM played dead,
All in the woodland early.
A PHEASANT and PARTRIDGE
Flew right past my head,
All in the woodland early.
I heard a loud QUAIL
As he took to his wings,
I saw a young RACCOON
And counted his rings,
All in the woodland early.

(To be spoken)
And where are you going this morning in May?
"We're going a-hunting," was all they would say.

(To be sung)
I saw a striped SKUNK
And I saw a small SHREW,
All in the woodland early;
A TURKEY came trotting
Right into my view,
All in the woodland early.
I saw an URBANUS,
A velvety VOLE,
And a very young WOODCHUCK
Just leaving his hole,
All in the woodland early.

(To be spoken)
And where are you going this morning in May?
"We're going a-hunting," was all they would say.

(To be sung)
I saw XYLEBORUS
Upon a tall tree,
All in the woodland early;
I heard YELLOW JACKET
A-buzzing near me,
All in the woodland early.
And last of all, ZEMMI,
Who's usually slow,
Ran out and went with them—
But where did they go,
All in the woodland early?

(To be spoken)
"Hunting, we're hunting," I heard them all say.
How *can* you go hunting on such a fine day?
"We're hunting for *friends!* Won't you come out and play,
All in the woodland early?"

The art for this book was prepared with a 000 brush,
watercolor and pencil on Opaline Parchment.
The typeface is Goudy Old Style set by Concept Typographic Services.